Perfection Learning®

Who Lives Here?

Helen Lepp Friesen

Table of Contents

Introduction 3
1. Prairie Dog's Burrow 4
2. Beaver's Lodge 6
3. Spiderweb 8
4. Bird's Nest 10
5. Fox's Den............................12
6. Beehive.................................13
7. Rabbit's Warren 14
Picture Glossary 16

Introduction

Animals have homes just like you and me. Homes keep animals dry and warm. Homes are a safe place to raise animal babies. Homes protect animals from enemies. Animals store food in their homes.

Chapter 1

Prairie Dog's Burrow

Who lives here?

Prairie dogs live in an underground home called a **burrow**. They dig long tunnels. In any weather, the burrow stays warm and dry.

Chapter 2

Beaver's Lodge

Beavers build **lodges** on rivers and lakes. They use their teeth to cut down trees. With branches and mud, beavers make their lodges. An underground tunnel leads to the front door.

Do I live here?

Chapter 3

Spiderweb

A spider makes its web from silky thread. It pushes the thread out through the back of its body. The web is a spider's home and also a trap for catching food.

An insect gets caught in the **spiderweb**. The spider wraps it in silk. Then the spider kills the insect and sucks out the juice.

Chapter 4

Bird's Nest

Birds build **nests** with small twigs and grass. They build them in trees or other safe places. Mother birds lay eggs in the nest.

Chapter 5

Do I live here?

Fox's Den

In the fall, fox families look for a home. They find a **den** in a hollow log or empty burrow. The den protects them from the cold winter. Mothers take care of the babies. Fathers find food for their families.

Chapter 6

Do I live here?

Beehive

Honeybees live in big groups. They build a home called a **hive**. The queen bee lays one egg in each small room, or cell. The eggs hatch. The new bees build new cells. They gather food for the queen bee.

Chapter 7

Do I live here?

Rabbit's Warren

Rabbits live together in a **warren**. They dig tunnels underground that connect small rooms. A warren is like an apartment building underground.

Picture Glossary

burrow

den

hive

lodge

nest

spiderweb

warren

Discovering Science

Leveled content-area science books in Earth/Space Science, Life Science, Math in Science, Physical Science, Science and Technology, and Science as Inquiry for emergent, early, and fluent readers

Who Lives Here?
Written by Helen Lepp Friesen

Text © 2007 by Perfection Learning® Corporation

All rights reserved. No part of this book may be reproduced, stored in a retrieval system, or transmitted in any form or by any means, electronic, mechanical, photocopying, recording, or otherwise, without prior permission of the publisher.

Printed in the United States of America.

For information, contact
Perfection Learning® Corporation
1000 North Second Avenue, P.O. Box 500
Logan, Iowa 51546-0500
Phone: 1-800-831-4190
Fax: 1-800-543-2745

perfectionlearning.com

PB ISBN 0-7891-6714-x

1 2 3 4 5 6 BA 11 10 09 08 07 06

Book Design: Robin Elwick

Photo Credits:

©Corbis Royalty-Free: pp. 10, 11, 16 (nest); iStock: front cover, pp. 4, 5, 7, 8–9, 9, 13 (right), 14, 15, 16 (burrow, hive, warren, spiderweb); Photos.com: back cover, pp. 3, 6–7, 12, 13 (left), 16 (den, lodge); Sue F. Cornelison: (ant) pp. 3, 5, 7, 9, 11, 12, 13, 14, 15; Robin Elwick: grass illustrations